P9-DHF-928

This book belongs to

Geoffrey

Young Readers Book Club presents...

I Had a Cat

by Mona Rabun Reeves

illustrated by Julie Downing

Bradbury Press　New York

To Alisha, Brandon, Christi,
Crystal, and Jennifer
—M.R.R.

To Judy
—J.D.

Text copyright © 1989 by Mona Rabun Reeves

Illustrations copyright © 1989 by Julie Downing

All rights reserved. No part of this book may be reproduced or transmitted in any form or by any means, electronic or mechanical, including photocopying, recording, or by any information storage and retrieval system, without permission in writing from the Publisher.

Bradbury Press
An Affiliate of Macmillan, Inc.
866 Third Avenue, New York, NY 10022
Collier Macmillan Canada, Inc.

A B C D   0 1 2 3

LIBRARY OF CONGRESS CATALOGING-IN-PUBLICATION DATA
Reeves, Mona R.
   I had a cat / by Mona R. Reeves; pictures by Julie Downing.
      p.   cm.
   Summary: The owner of a cat, dog, bird, ape, frog, elk, deer, and a multitude of other animals finds new homes for all but one.
   ISBN 0-02-775731-5
   [1. Animals—Fiction. 2. Stories in rhyme.] I. Downing, Julie, ill. II. Title.   PZ8.3.R263Iah 1989
[E]—dc19   87-37608   CIP   AC

Grolier Enterprises Inc. offers a varied selection of children's book racks and tote bags. For details on ordering, please write: Grolier Enterprises Inc., Sherman Turnpike, Danbury, CT 06816 Attn: Premium Department

I had a cat.

I had a dog.

I had a bird, an ape,
A frog.

I had an elk, a deer, a moose.

I had a really silly goose.

I had a fish. I had a bear.
I had a whale, a sheep, a hare.

I had a wolf, a goat, an ox,
A skunk, a yak, a fuzzy fox.
I had a horse, a calf, a cow.

I had a bull, a pig, a sow.
I had a pair of furry minks,
A seal, a snake, a mole, a lynx.
To top it off, I had a ram,
A duck, a hen, a snow-white lamb.

There was no room left in the house,
Not even for a tiny mouse.
There was no food left in the shed.
The animals could not be fed.
I did not know what else to do;

I paid a visit to the zoo.

I said, "Hello." And "How are you?"
And "Would you like a beast or two?"

They took the ape, the elk, the moose,
The deer, the bear, the silly goose.
They took the whale, the wolf, the minks,
The yak, the skunk, the fox, the lynx.
They also took the seal and snake.
But that was all that they could take.
I thanked the people at the zoo
And said good-bye. They thanked me, too.

I went in search of Farmer Brown.
I found him at the edge of town.
I said, "Hello." And "How are you?"

And "Would you like a beast or two?"
He took the horse, the dog, the cow,
The calf, the bull, the pig and sow.

He took the sheep, the goat, the ram,
The ox, the duck, the hen, the lamb.
He tipped his hat and said, "Thank you."
I wished him well, and thanked him, too.

I met a boy along the road
Who traveled with a large green toad.
I said, "Hello." And "How are you?"
and "Would you like a beast or two?"

He took the frog without a word;
He took the fish, the hare, the bird.
He smiled and waved to say good-bye.
He said, "Thank you," and so did I.

Into the ground I dug a hole;
Inside I put the happy mole.
The mole was free, and so was I.
I turned around.

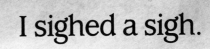

I sighed a sigh.

I went back home.
The house looked bare,

Until I saw her on the chair.
I smiled.
She purred as there she sat…

I was so glad I had a cat.